EXIT
THE BOOK OF SECRET NOTES
MEOW MEOW
SLOW
SCHOOL
POLICE
JUICE

EXIT
SLOW
SCHOOL
REPORT CARD
MEOW MEOW
ORANGE JUICE
GRAPE
POLICE
SMASHING
P

David Mortimore Baxter

The Truth!

by Karen Tayleur

illustrated by Brann Garvey

Librarian Reviewer
Kathleen Baxter
Children's Literature Consultant
formerly with Anoka County Library, MN
BA College of Saint Catherine, St. Paul, MN
MA in Library Science, University of Minnesota

Reading Consultant
Elizabeth Stedem
Educator/Consultant, Colorado Springs, CO
MA in Elementary Education, University of Denver, CO

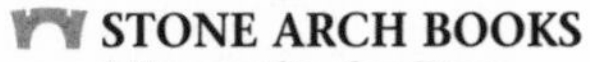

STONE ARCH BOOKS
Minneapolis San Diego

First published in the United States in 2007
by Stone Arch Books, A Capstone Imprint
151 Good Counsel Drive, P.O. Box 669,
Mankato, Minnesota 56002
www.capstonepub.com

Published by arrangement with Black Dog Books.

Library of Congress Cataloging-in-Publication Data
Tayleur, Karen.
The Truth!: David Mortimore Baxter Comes Clean / by Karen Tayleur; illustrated by Brann Garvey.
p. cm. — (David Mortimore Baxter)
Summary: Caught "bending the truth" again, young David Mortimore Baxter decides to follow a strict diet of honesty which lands him in more trouble.
ISBN-13: 978-1-59889-078-5 (hardcover)
ISBN-10: 1-59889-078-6 (hardcover)
ISBN-13: 978-1-59889-210-9 (paperback)
ISBN-10: 1-59889-210-X (paperback)
[1. Honesty—Fiction. 2. Humorous stories.] I. Garvey, Brann, ill. II. Title. III. Title: David Mortimore Baxter comes clean. IV. Series: Tayleur, Karen. David Mortimore Baxter.
PZ7.T21149Tr 2007
[Fic]—dc22 2006005078

Art Director: Heather Kindseth
Graphic Designer: Kay Fraser

Photo Credits
Delaney Photography, cover

Printed in the United States of America in Stevens Point, Wisconsin.
072013
007610R

Table of Contents

CHAPTER 1

KIDNAPPED

Saturday, August 8

Hi. I'm David Mortimore Baxter. You're probably wondering why I'm locked up in the cabin of a luxury cruiser. Well, it's more like an old boat. You might also wonder why my friends **Joe Pagnopolous**, **Bec Trigg**, and Bec's pet rat, **Ralph**, are here with me.

I'm not sure who locked us in. It could have been **kidnappers**. Or **robbers**. Or **pirates**. Joe said it might have been aliens, but Bec pointed out they would probably use spaceships.

The TRUTH is, I can't see any way out of this. It's the truth, because that's all I'm allowed to tell now. **The truth. The whole truth. And nothing but.** And look where it got me.

This has been the worst week of my life.

CHAPTER 2

SICK OF ROSE

Saturday, August 1

It all started a week ago. **I got caught telling a lie**. Again. The truth is, I had a lying habit. I lied because sometimes the truth can be boring.

Anyway, last Saturday night Mom **snapped,** and it was all Rose Thornton's fault.

Rose is my **worst enemy**. I don't hate her, because Mom says I'm not allowed to hate anybody. **So I really, really, really don't like Rose**. Rose doesn't like me either. She always thinks I'm telling lies. Or that I'm just about to tell a lie. Or that I'm thinking about telling a lie. She calls me **Larry Liar**. Larry for short. It's a pretty stupid joke.

On Saturday, my family was invited to the Thorntons' house for dinner. I **didn't** want to go. My dad and Mr. Thornton have known each other forever.

They went to school together. I think that's the ONLY thing they have in common.

Anyway, my sister, Zoe, was staying home to do a biology project or something. That meant there was someone at home to watch me if I could come up with a **good enough reason**. So I **pretended to be sick**. I LAY on my bed and WAITED for Mom to find me.

Boris lay down on the floor next to me and began to PANT. I don't know why he was **faking it**. He didn't have to go to the Thorntons'.

At home, Boris is like my **shadow**. When I turned four, Dad gave me Boris as a birthday gift. Dad had seen him in a pet store window on the way home from work. The next thing he knew, he was asking, "*How much is that doggy in the window?*" Then he was **taking him home**. Mom didn't think I was old enough to have a dog, but Dad insisted and Boris stayed. Boris has always been **slow** and **slobbery**.

"Come on, David. Let's go. We're running late."

Mom had finally come looking for me. I **groaned**. I **moaned**. I **rolled around** a little on the bed.

Mom sighed and left the room. She came back with a **thermometer** and stuck it in **my mouth**. Then she left the room to give instructions for the night to my sister.

I grabbed the thermometer out of my mouth and shoved it into **BORIS'S** **open mouth.** By the time Mom was back I'd taken the thermometer from Boris and was handing it to her. She looked at the temperature, frowned, and then shook it. Huge chunks of Boris spit flew off it.

"I'm not sure that this is working," Mom said. "Let's try it again. Open your mouth."

Then I really did feel sick. I thought I might throw up. There was no way I wanted that thing in my mouth after Boris had it in his. I must have looked sick too, because Mom suddenly looked **worried**. **LUCKILY** she forgot about the thermometer.

"David, maybe we should cancel tonight and we'll all stay home. I'll just call the Thorntons and reschedule," she said.

"**No**," I said, sitting up in bed quickly. That meant that we'd have to go to the Thorntons' another time for dinner. "No," I said, lying down again. "I'll be fine here with Zoe. **I'll probably just sleep.**"

"Well, I'm not sure about this."

"Mom, really. There's no point in everyone staying home." I gave her a **brave smile**.

"All right. I'll leave the Thorntons' phone number with Zoe in case she needs to call us. Now, you get into *your pajamas* and hop under the covers. I'll check on you when we get back." Then she **patted my cheek softly**. That's when I felt like a **JERK**.

My brother Harry came in before they left. "You're not sick," he said. "What am I going to do at the Thorntons' without you? They'll probably want me to hang out with Rose or something."

I waved at him. "Give Rose a kiss for me," I said.

Harry looked like he was going to **punch** me. I was saved when Dad called out, "Come on, Harry."

Harry headed for the door. He gave me a WEIRD little smile.

I should have paid more attention to that smile. But I was just happy that I didn't have to hang out with Rose Thornton.

After the family left, Zoe stuck her head through my bedroom doorway. "Sick?" she asked.

"**Nope**," I said.

"Cool," she answered. Then she left. I heard her bedroom door slam. I probably wouldn't see her for the rest of the night.

I went to the kitchen and grabbed a **few snacks**. The cookie jar was only half full, so I got a bag of chips too. Then I decided to play Spies in my bedroom with Boris.

Spies is a game that Joe and Bec and I made up one rainy weekend. It's all about strategy. There are **two things** you can do when you are a SPY. The **first thing** is **gather information. The second thing is creep up** on someone and catch them by surprise.

The point is being quiet enough to get Maximum Surprise Value. **Maximum Surprise Value** (or MSV, as Bec calls it) is one of Joe's ideas. He probably got it from a movie. (Joe is addicted to movies. His family owns a video store and he wants to be an actor.)

I decided to make a spy headquarters. I grabbed the pillows and blanket off my bed and dumped them on the floor. I stacked the pillows and my beanbag from the corner of my room, then put the blanket on top. This made **a great mountain**.

It was pretty hard work building a mountain. I grabbed some drink from the kitchen. By the time I got back to my room, Boris had made a tunnel through the mountain. He'd stuck his head under the blanket and walked in.

"**Get out of there, Captain Boris**. You're messing up the location! That is not MSV," I said.

I **CRAWLED** in under the blanket and found Boris munching on some potato chips.

"Those are the rations. **You're not supposed to be eating these yet!**" I yelled. I grabbed the bag out of Boris's mouth and fell backward. Chips flew through the air and Boris scrambled over me to get to them.

That's when I realized **I had company**.

"*David Mortimore Baxter*!" The voice came from out of nowhere.

I looked over at my bedroom doorway. I wasn't alone. I thought about that weird little smile Harry had given me before he left. He obviously was making me pay for staying home without him.

Rose Thornton was shaking her head. And Mom was looming over both of them.

"*You've really done it this time, David,*" she said.

CHAPTER 3

THE TRUTH

(Sat.-Sun.), August 1-2

I'm sure Rose wanted to hang around for the **fireworks**. Mom had other ideas. She told Rose and Harry to get back into the car.

"I'm glad to see you've *recovered* from your illness *so quickly*," said Mom. "Harry was very concerned about you being sick and Rose came to cheer you up."

"I—" I began.

"Don't bother, David. I want you to clean up this mess. Then I *want you to finish your math homework*."

"But that's **not due until Tuesday**!"

"I'll check it when I come home. When you have *finished your homework*, **go to bed**. *We will discuss this tomorrow*. I think your father will want to talk to you." She looked at Boris. "And put that dog in the laundry room."

Boris only went in the laundry room if he'd done something wrong. Mom must have been really mad. When she left, I grabbed Boris by the collar and led him to the laundry room.

"**Sorry, buddy**. You have to stay here for now," I said, closing the door in his face.

I pulled my math homework out and worked on some problems at the kitchen table. I wanted to call Joe or Bec, but I figured that would probably just get me into more trouble. After half an hour, Zoe came into the kitchen, went to the fridge, and poured herself a drink.

"Juice, **Dribbles?**" she asked me. Dribbles was her nickname for me. I never let anyone else call me that.

I shook my head.

"You in **trouble**?" she asked.

I nodded.

"Too bad," she said. Then she took the juice carton back to her bedroom and slammed the door.

Zoe wouldn't win any awards for public speaking, but she always knew how to make me feel better. That's when she wasn't making my life miserable.

After I finished my homework, I went to bed and turned out the light.

* * *

In the morning I woke up with that good "**Sunday, no school today!**" feeling. Then I remembered the night before and I felt sick. Not that I'd tell Mom. She wouldn't believe me ever again.

After breakfast I washed the dishes. Then I went to my room to stay out of everyone's way. Unfortunately, Mom and Dad **knew where to find me**. When they finally both came into my room, I was kind of relieved. **Waiting** to be punished was almost **WORSE** than the punishment itself.

Or so I thought at the time.

"*We need to have a talk*," began Mom, as they sat down on the end of my bed. She went on and on about me being a liar and how **she was so disappointed with me**.

She talked for at least ten minutes without taking one breath. I wanted to time her breathing on my bedroom clock.

I wondered **how long you would have to hold your breath** if you wanted to be one of those people who dived for pearls. I'd seen a movie the week before with Joe, and there was this giant squid that snuck up on a diver.

"So what do you have to say about that?" asked Mom.

I'd actually stopped listening about five minutes earlier, so I played it safe.

"**That's fair**," I said.

Dad raised his eyebrows. "Really, David? I'm surprised," he said.

UH oh. I had obviously **missed** out on a **vital piece of information.**

"So that's settled," said Mom. "From now on it's the truth, the whole truth, and nothing but the truth. *Or Boris goes to the pound.*"

What? Were they kidding? I looked at my parents. There was no hint of a smile.

Boris. My dog. In a pound? They couldn't do that. There must be a law against it, or something I could do.

"I just hope you learn something from this," said Mom.

I thought LONG and HARD about what she said. I didn't want to get it wrong.

"I don't think so," I answered truthfully.

"And that answer means **no television** for a week," said Dad as he left the room.

Telling the truth was going to be hard work.

CHAPTER 4

THE BORIS PROBLEM

Monday, August 3

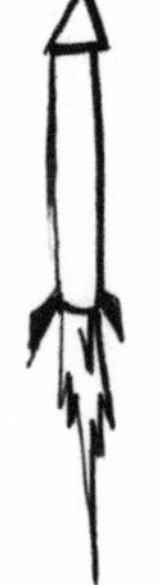

The next day was Monday. At recess I told BEC and JOE about my weekend.

"**Wow, that's harsh**," said Joe. At least, I think that's what he said. Joe was always dressing up as his latest favorite movie character. That week it was either an astronaut or motorcycle hero. He was wearing a motorcycle helmet covered in tin foil. It was hard to hear him.

Bec seemed pretty quiet.

"**Well?**" I asked her.

"I guess something BAD was bound to happen," said Bec.

If ever you want a **truthful** answer, just ask Bec. I couldn't count on Bec to make me feel better. If she thought I was wrong, she would always tell me.

"**What?**" I said.

"Well, you do tell lies, David. You'd be lying if you said you didn't," said Bec.

"Yeah, but **taking Boris away from me**? Do you think that's **FAIR**, Bec?" I asked.

"**No**," she said. "Your mom must have been **really mad**. And **embarrassed**."

"**What?**" I asked.

"Well, she went to the Thorntons' house for dinner. She told them you were sick. Then **Rose found out** you were faking it, and the Thorntons obviously found out."

"**Rose Thornton**!" I said.

"Rose Thornton," said Joe, nodding his head in slow motion. He was obviously an astronaut. Or a really slow motorcyclist.

"You **CAN'T** really blame Rose," began Bec.

"Because of Rose, I'm going to lose my dog. **What is it with her?** Does she hate me so much that she'd pick on a **defenseless dog?**"

Just then, Rose walked by with her *Giggling Girls*, or the **GG's**, as I liked to call them.

" He's worth millions. Actually, I'm inviting someone really special to my party. Don't ask me who, it's a surprise," Rose was saying.

Mrs. Thornton worked in PR, whatever that was. It was the kind of job where she met lots of stars and rich people. Rose was always babbling about it.

"What kind of monster are you?" I yelled.

Rose turned around. "*Feeling better, Larry?*" she asked. The GG's HONKED and HOOTED with **laughter** as they walked off.

"**I'm really mad now!**"

"**Don't, David**," said Bec. "Getting even with Rose isn't going to help you keep Boris. I think we need a **Secret Club meeting**. My place after school?"

I nodded, then pointed to Joe, who was walking in slow motion after Rose. He was taking this astronaut thing too far.

"**What are you doing, Joe**?" I called out to him.

"I'm going to tell Rose Thornton **what I think of her,**" he answered.

"Forget it," said Bec. "By the time you reach her, she'll be an old woman."

Then the bell rang and it was time to go inside.

* * *

After school we met under the basement stairs at Bec's apartment. This was the closest thing we had to an official **Secret Club hideout**. When we were playing spies, it was also our **spy base**.

Bec had only found the space recently. It was just big enough for the three of us to fit into. The floor was dusty and there was a weak light bulb, just strong enough to write by.

It was an official **Secret Club meeting**, so Bec had the Club Book with her. Bec was the keeper of the book. She recorded every meeting. Bec also had her pet rat, Ralph, who was peeking out from her pocket. RALPH the rat often went on adventures in Bec's pocket. He was an honorary Secret Club member.

"I call this meeting of the Secret Club **to order**," I began. "**Joe, take that helmet off.**"

Joe shook his head. "Can't. **No oxygen**. Alien atmosphere." He was obviously still in space.

"Okay, we're here today to **talk about Rose Thornton**," I began.

Bec put down her pen. "**No**, we're not," she said. "We're here to talk about your 'losing Boris' problem. You can't blame Rose for everything."

Joe nodded in agreement. Slowly. "**Roger that**," he said.

"**Who's Roger?**" I asked.

"Astronaut speak. He agrees," said Bec, scribbling something in the book.

"**Copy that**," said Joe.

"**That's it**," I said.

I reached over and pulled the helmet off Joe's head. He grabbed at his throat. He gasped for air, then sank to the ground. **On a scale of one to ten, his pretend death was a three.**

Ralph hopped out of Bec's pocket to investigate dead Joe.

"Forget it, David. Look, I don't see any way out of this. You're just going to have to start telling the truth," said Bec.

"I do tell the **truth**!"

"**All the time**," said Bec.

"Maybe I could just **try** telling the truth **all the time at home?**" I suggested.

Bec shook her head. "Your mom will find out. Besides, telling lies at school usually affects what happens to you at home," she said. "Remember Smashing Smorgan?"

How could I forget? I lied to Rose Thornton that Smashing Smorgan was coming to my place for lunch, and the whole class came to my house to see him. In the end I did meet Smashing Smorgan, but he told me how bad I'd been. As punishment, I had cleaned his dressing room while everyone else **got to watch him in action at Wicked Wrestling Mania.**

What Bec and Joe didn't know was that I'd invited Smashing Smorgan to sail around the bay on Dad's luxury cruiser. The only problem was that **Dad didn't own a luxury cruiser**. I still hadn't found a solution to that problem.

Maybe Bec **was right**. Maybe I needed to **STOP my lies.**

"Okay," I said. "**No more lies.**"

Joe raised his hand slowly and gave me a no-gravity high five.

"This will solve all your problems," Bec said.

Unfortunately, she was wrong.

CHAPTER 5

IN TROUBLE

Tuesday, August 4

The next morning I got up early. I hadn't had a good night's sleep. I was too busy trying to figure out when a lie was a lie and when it might be something else. Sometimes I bent the truth. Just a little bend. But those lies just grew and grew until it got totally out of hand.

The way I saw it, the **only way to go was complete honesty.**

I got ready for school, and then explained to Boris that his life at the **Baxter house** was only possible while I told no lies. I **PROMISED** to do my best to keep him. I had to keep poking him to get his attention. He began snoring. He was **obviously overwhelmed by stress.**

I knew it was going to be a **bad day** when Zoe shuffled into the kitchen. Zoe doesn't really wake up until after 10 o'clock, so I usually try to stay away from her. Until she wakes up she's like a GRUMPY bear that **just came out of hibernation.**

"What do you think?" she mumbled.

"**About what?**" I said, my mouth full of cereal.

"My hair. It cost me all of my birthday money. Sixty bucks."

"**Oh,**" I said.

"So, what do you think?" she growled.

I looked at her hair. I thought about my new life with no lies. "**I think it looks the same as it always looked,**" I said.

"What?" Zoe growled, now fully awake. "Are you blind? *You moron*. Why did I ask you? *You have no idea.*" She stormed into her bedroom and slammed the door shut. That was **Zoe's first slammed** door for the day. I keep score. Her best was ten door slams when she wasn't allowed to get her eyebrow pierced.

SLAM!

"I think it looks good, Zoe," Harry called out as he sat down to eat some breakfast.

"Idiot," I said.

"Slimeball," he answered.

"Moron."

"Takes one to know one," Harry answered. That was his favorite comeback.

Just another morning in the **Baxter house**.

"What was that about?" demanded Dad as he hurried through the kitchen.

"David said Zoe's hair looked dumb," said Harry.

"No I didn't," I said. I kicked Harry under the table.

"Eat your cereal, Harry," said Mom, on her way to the fridge. "It's your favorite."

"I hate this cereal," said Harry. "And so does David."

"That's *not true*," said Mom. "David *loves* that cereal. Don't you, David?"

I had hoped she wasn't going to ask me that. My head sunk as I shoveled another mouthful in.

"David?" repeated Mom.

I swallowed my food and looked her in the eye. "**No,**" I answered truthfully.

"What?" she demanded.

"No. I don't love this cereal. **I don't even like it.**"

"But it's got oats and bran," she said, sounding like a **TV commercial**. "It's got chopped fruit. There's no added sugar. *Since when haven't you liked this cereal, David?*"

"**Since you started buying it,**" I answered.

"But you told me you liked it," said Mom, looking confused.

"You asked me if I liked it and I said yes. **I didn't want to hurt your feelings.** But you want me to tell the **truth** now, so I am."

"Okay," she said. She went out to the back garden, slamming the door behind her.

Dad walked into the kitchen again. "What was that?" he asked.

"Mom," Harry said. "She's mad at David because he doesn't like the cereal."

"You seem to be causing some TROUBLE today, young man," said Dad.

You have to be careful when Dad calls you a young man. It usually means you're in trouble.

If I hung around Harry any more, **Boris** and **I** would both end up at the pound. I mumbled something about being full, and headed out. The sooner I got to school, the better.

* * *

At school, things did not get better. When our teacher, Ms. Stacey, asked for our math homework sheets, I GROANED.

"What's wrong, **Mission Control**?" asked Joe. He wasn't wearing his space helmet today, but he was obviously still an astronaut.

"I left my worksheet at home," I answered.

"Oh. This should not affect your mission," said Joe. "You ALWAYS leave your worksheet at home."

"But I actually did the homework!"

"Oh. Too bad. I mean, copy that," said Joe.

Ms. Stacey walked around the desks collecting the worksheets. When she came to me, she **stopped** and **waited**.

I never have my worksheet on Tuesday mornings. Some weeks I hand it in on Friday. Some weeks I don't hand it in at all. But every week I have an excuse for not having it ready on Tuesday. I think Ms. Stacey admires the effort I put into my excuses. She told me if I spent as much time doing my homework as I did making excuses for not doing it, **I'd be a genius**.

"Well, David?" she asked.

"I left my worksheet at home, Ms. Stacey." She looked disappointed.

"Is that the BEST you can do?" she said.

"It's true," I answered. "I finished all my homework by Saturday night, but I forgot my sheet today."

She just shook her head. "I preferred the excuse about your backpack being stolen," she said as she walked away. "That's a RECESS detention for you, David Baxter."

"But I really did do my homework. It's the **truth**," I insisted.

"Would you like to make that TWO *detentions*?" asked Ms. Stacey.

"Here's my worksheet, Ms. Stacey," said Rose Thornton sweetly. "I did some extra problems on the back."

"*Good work*, Rose," said Ms. Stacey.

I looked at Bec, who was making silent **gagging** faces behind Ms. Stacey's back. **She really, really didn't like Rose Thornton**. Almost as much as I didn't. I LAUGHED out loud when Bec made a **really good face**.

"Okay, *David Baxter*. Please *stand up* and tell the class what is *so funny*," said Ms. Stacey, glaring at me.

Bec's eyes grew wide with ALARM. She knew the new David Mortimore Baxter **couldn't tell a lie**.

"We're waiting, David," said Ms. Stacey.

I stood up. I do some of my best story telling when I'm in trouble. Thirty kids were waiting for one of my fantastic stories, but I had to tell the truth this time. Bec was shaking her head. Rose Thornton was leaning forward with interest.

"Come on, Larry," whispered Rose.

Joe whispered, "**Alien atmosphere**," and in a flash I knew what to do. I closed my eyes and fell to the floor. On a scale of one to ten, I'd say **my pretend death rated at least a five.**

CHAPTER 6

SICK OF LYING

I hung around the **nurse's office** for a while and waited for things to **COOL** down. I was still trying to decide if my **pretend faint** counted as a lie. I hadn't said I fainted. I'd just pretended. So that was okay. I didn't actually **LIE**. Boris was safe for now.

Mrs. Schtick was having a hard time with her computer. **She ignored me completely.** Mrs. Schtick was the school nurse, but it seemed like sick kids really **interfered** with her day. She'd looked **pretty annoyed** to see me when I'd limped into her office.

She finally gave up on her computer, grabbed her notebook, and came to see me.

"*Medication?*" she asked.

"**What?**"

"Are you on *any medication*? Do you have *asthma*? Are you *allergic to anything*?"

I **SHRUGGED**. "**Don't you have all that info?**" I asked.

"*Of course* I do," she snapped. "But it's not all up here," she said, pointing to her head. "I have to *check the computer and the server is down.*"

"**Oh,**" I said. I knew how the server felt. I was pretty down too.

"Honestly," she went on. "Do you think I have *nothing better to do* than to ask you questions all day?"

"**Honestly?**" I answered. "**No.**"

"What did you say?" she said.

"**NO**, I **don't think you have anything better to do.**" Then I stopped. She probably hadn't expected an answer.

"Why, you are so . . ."

"**Rude?**" I offered.

She nodded.

"**Terrible, bad boy?**" I said. These were all the words that Mr. McCafferty, my neighbor, used when he was talking about me.

Mrs. Schtick just nodded again.

"You are **so mad** at me that you are going to **get the principal?**" I suggested.

Mrs. Schtick **RUSHED** from the room.

Ms. Stacey appeared a few minutes later. Mrs. Schtick must have run all the way to the principal.

"Are you feeling better, Mr. Baxter?" she asked briskly.

"**Yes, Ms. Stacey,**" I answered. It was true. At least I wasn't standing up in front of a crowd of students about to tell on my friend.

"Did you really faint, David, or **were you just pretending?"**

"**Just pretending**, Ms. Stacey," I said **truthfully**.

She looked a little **SHOCKED** that I'd told her the truth.

"**How did you know?**" I asked her.

"You fainted one day when you ran out of homework excuses," said Ms. Stacey. "Although, this faint was a lot better than your first one. Well, if you're better, you can come back to class and take the **math test**," she said, scribbling a note for Mrs. Schtick.

For once I was glad to take a math test.

* * *

"That was a **close call**, Commander Baxter," said Joe, as we sat under the oak tree at lunchtime.

"Copy that!" I answered.

"*Thanks*, David," said Bec. "I *almost died* when Ms. Stacey asked you to stand up in class."

"Me too," I said. "Telling the truth **all the time** is killing me. I just don't know if I can keep it up."

"You **have** to," said Joe. "For our fellow space traveler, Boris Baxter."

A shadow fell over us. I looked up and saw Rose Thornton.

"*What's going on?*" she demanded. "You're acting **WEIRD**, *even for you*, Larry."

"Mission Control, **we have a problem**," said Joe, talking into a rock.

"I know it's *something* to do with last Saturday night," said Rose.

"An **alien life form**," said Joe into his rock. "**Possibly dangerous**."

"I don't know what it is, but I'm going to find out," continued Rose, ignoring Joe. "*Then you'll be sorry.*"

"Why don't you go annoy someone else," said Bec with a scowl. "What is your problem, Rose?"

"*My problem?*" said Rose. She put her hands on her hips. "I think you know what my problem is. *First, David's stupid dog ruins* my new pair of designer **jeans**. *Then he ruins the dog show* so that my poor dog Tiffany doesn't win a prize. *Then David ruins my role in the school play*. Who knows what *talent scout was in the audience* that night! I am **never** going to forgive you for that, David. **Never!**" Then she stormed away.

"**But that was weeks ago**," I said, shaking my head.

You can say one thing for Rose. **She sure can hold a GRUDGE.**

CHAPTER 7

SPIES

That afternoon after school, Joe and Bec came over to my place. We **hung out in the park for a while.** **Joe had suggested** a **game of Spies**, so we were using our spying skills on my neighbor, Mr. McCafferty.

Mr. McCafferty was going to be out of a job now that I'd stopped lying. He was always calling my parents about something bad I'd done. When he called last Sunday night, Mom told him that I wouldn't be telling any more lies.

"Do you have the **suspect** in sight?" asked Bec, who was ready to write down details in her notebook.

"**Yes**," replied Joe. "He is still **attacking** the plants with a sharp weapon."

The only thing Joe had spied on so far was Mr. McCafferty pruning his roses. I was about to call it quits when the sound of one hundred **honking geese** announced that the **GG's** were nearby.

"That's the GG's," I whispered.

"Yes, **space cadet**," said Joe. "And they have their leader with them. The Thorned Rose."

"What are they doing here?" asked Bec, writing down the name Rose in her Spy notebook.

"Hard to say," said Joe. "They appear to **be friends of Alien McCafferty**."

"**Friends?**" I asked. Since when had Rose Thornton and Mr. McCafferty been friends? I grabbed the binoculars from Joe's hand and stood up, **staying close to the tree**.

Sure enough, it was Rose Thornton and her Giggling Girls, who had stopped to talk to Mr. McCafferty. I didn't need the binoculars to tell me that. But why would they be talking to Mr. McCafferty?

Rose was patting Mr. Figgins, Mr. McCafferty's **nasty cat**, and giving Mr. McCafferty a cheesy smile.

What was she up to?

"**Anything to report?**" asked Bec.

I focused my binoculars on **Rose's lips**. They looked like two wet slugs doing a dance. I wished I could **read lips**.

"I think it's **time to retreat** to base," I said. "We're **NOT** going to learn anything here."

I took one last look at Rose's smiling face and felt a **shiver** start at **my shoulders and work its way down to my toes**. It was like looking into the face of a **rattlesnake** just before it strikes.

At my house, we decided to have a **Secret Club meeting**, although Bec didn't have the Club Book. At the table, Joe moved his helmet visor up so he could **push cookies into his mouth** through the gap.

Bec drew two circles in her notebook. In one circle she wrote, "*Rose*." In the second circle, she wrote, "*Mr. McCafferty*."

"If we were **real spies**, we would try to solve today's mystery," said Bec. "*Why* was Rose talking to Mr. McCafferty?"

"**Coincidence**?" suggested Joe.

Bec wrote "*coincidence*" on the notebook page.

Ralph had **POPPED** out from her pocket and was **chasing the pen across the page.**

"Maybe," said Bec.

I shook my head. "No way," I said. "**Rose is a mean little . . .**"

"**Space alien**," said Joe.

"**Yes**," I agreed. "I just **don't trust her**."

"We need to find out what Rose and Mr. McCafferty *have in common*," said Bec.

"They both have pets?" suggested Joe.

Bec wrote "*pets*."

"What else?" she asked.

"They're both **mean**?" I said.

"They **both pretend** to be nice to people?" said Joe.

"They **both don't like me?**" I said.

Bec nodded slowly then wrote "*David*" in the notebook. Then she underlined the word a couple of times.

"That's it," she said.

She tore off the page and gave it to me.

Rose Thornton and Mr. McCafferty were both out to get me. If they had joined forces, **things were about to get much worse**.

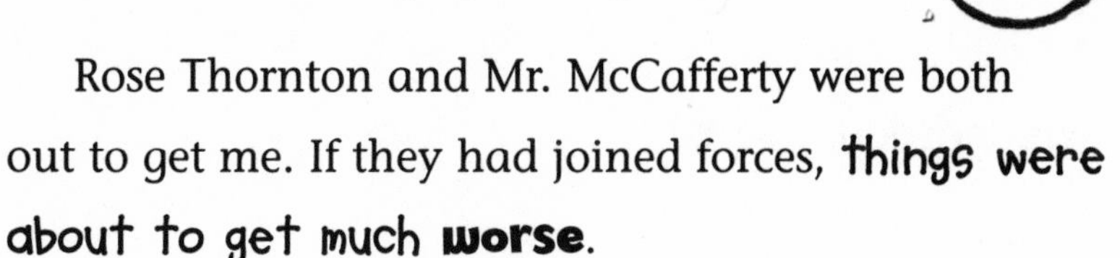

"**Now what?**" asked Joe, forcing another cookie through his visor gap.

"**I think the Secret Club Spies will be keeping a very close eye on Rose Thornton,**" I said as I dropped half a cookie into Boris's mouth.

CHAPTER 8

A BAD DAY

Wednesday, August 5

The next day was Wednesday. I spent the whole day telling the truth. **It almost killed me**. Actually, other people almost killed me. I **NEVER** realized **how often I lied**.

First there was Ms. Stacey. I got to school early for a change. Joe wasn't there yet, but Bec and I had a quick spies session before school. In the game, we were from different **spy agencies**. My spy base was the **oak tree** and Bec's was **the bike racks**. We started from our separate bases and needed to creep up on each other for **MSV**.

I couldn't see Bec anywhere. Suddenly I saw **a flash of color** through our classroom window. It looked like Bec was hiding inside the school, which **wasn't allowed** before the bell rang.

I guess she thought I'd never look there. She was going to be surprised when I found her.

I crept through the main entrance doors, up the hall, to our classroom door, which was shut. I listened carefully for a sign that she was inside. I heard the faint creak of a chair being sat on. She was still there.

I **swung** open the door quickly and **shouted**, "MSV!"

But there was no Bec. Instead, Ms. Stacey was sitting at her desk, holding a large poster, **her mouth open in surprise**.

"What? What?" she said.

"**Sorry, Ms. Stacey**," I said. "I thought you were Bec." I looked closer at the poster. "Is that **Smashing Smorgan**?"

Ms. Stacey's face turned as **RED** as a stop sign. She shoved the poster into her desk and slammed the drawer shut.

"*I had to take that poster from a student,*" she explained.

Everyone knows that Ms. Stacey has **a crush** on Smashing Smorgan, so **I didn't believe that for a second.**

"You don't think it's mine, *do you?*" she asked.

I nodded. "**Yes, Ms. Stacey. I do.**"

Then Ms. Stacey *gave me a lecture* about being inside the school before school and about not being rude to my elders. Then she said she'd be *calling my parents.*

During art, Rose and the **GG's** were huddled around Mrs. George's desk, **ooohhhing** and **ahhing**.

"What are **they** up to?" I asked Joe.

Joe just **SHRUGGED**. He wasn't talking to me.

I needed to ask Mrs. George a question, but the girls were there. I walked up to her desk, hoping they'd leave.

"Oh, *show David*, Mrs. George," said Rose sweetly. "He'd love to see."

Mrs. George reached into her drawer and pulled out a small photo album. She opened the album and shoved it in front of me. "Isn't he gorgeous?" she asked.

At first I couldn't figure out what it was. It looked like some kind of **hairless monkey**. Its face was all **SQUISHED** up **from crying**. Its skin was red and flaky like it had been left out in the sun too long. It didn't seem to have a body, just a **HEAD** and a **blue blanket**.

"**My first grandson**," explained Mrs. George. "Isn't he **beautiful?**"

I wished she hadn't asked me that. **Why do people call new babies beautiful?** It was the ugliest baby I had ever seen, and I'd seen a lot. It was even **uglier than my brother, Harry**, had been. Zoe told me once that there were hardly any photos of Harry because whenever someone tried to take a photo of him, his face broke the camera.

"Well?" insisted Rose. "Isn't he *adorable*, David?"

I had **walked into a trap**. Mrs. George and the GG's looked at me.

I was going to have to tell the truth. Suddenly, there was a CRASH and a HOWL. Bec had dropped a pot of blue paint onto the sink and it had splashed straight up the wall.

"Sorry, Mrs. George. It was an accident," said Bec.

"**Just clean it up, Rebecca.**" Mrs. George raced off to get some paper towels.

"*I'm watching you, David Baxter,*" whispered Rose.

CHAPTER 9

A VISIT TO THE PRINCIPAL

Wednesday, Aug. 5

During music I made Mrs. Tozer mad. That was too bad, because **I really like her, even though she is a terrible music teacher**. She is the only person I know who sings **worse than my dad**. When Dad sings, **Boris howls like he's in PAIN**.

"This is a new song, class, so I'm going to sing the chorus and I'll get each of you to repeat it after me. *David, you first,*" said Mrs. Tozer, smiling at me.

Mrs. Tozer sang the chorus. "Now you try, David."

I copied Mrs. Tozer exactly. Where she'd gone up, I went up. Where she'd gone down, **I went down**. Where her voice **wobbled**, my voice wobbled. Before I finished, **the class was laughing** and Mrs. Tozer asked me to **STOP**.

"That's enough, David. *Please sing it just like I did.*"

"But I did, Mrs. Tozer. Honest."

Rose Thornton's hand shot up in the air. "Let me, Mrs. Tozer. I'll do it."

"Thank you, Rose. Sit down, David." Mrs. Tozer ignored me for the rest of the lesson.

In gym class that afternoon, our class wasn't paying too much attention to our teacher, Mr. Mildendew. Finally, Mr. Moldy (our nickname for him) asked us if we thought he was talking just to hear the sound of his own voice. I was the only one who said yes.

Bleeep, bleeep, bleeep went the whistle.

"Principal's office!" shouted Mr. Mildendew.

I'd been waiting to hear those words all day.

* * *

After school, my plan was to stay in my room until Boris and I died of old age. I figured I'd save Mom the trouble of grounding me.

Zoe came in and told me there were two messages from the school on the answering machine.

"I don't think *Mom's heard them yet,*" she said helpfully.

"**It's just a matter of time,**" I said, patting Boris.

Harry came in. He actually looked **WORRIED** for once.

"**Hi, Slimeball,**" he said.

"**Idiot.**"

"Takes one to know one," he said automatically. "Are you going to **lose Boris**?"

"**Probably,**" I said. "If I don't get in trouble for telling lies, I'll **get in trouble for telling the truth.**"

"I didn't know **Mom would be so mad**!"

I wanted to yell at Harry and tell him it was all **his fault** that Boris would be sent to the pound. **But something stopped me**. Maybe it was that he looked so **SAD**. Like he might **burst into tears or something**. Maybe it was that I knew that it **was really my own fault.**

Later, Bec called to suggest that we **spy** on Rose Thornton the next day. "*You never know*, we might find out something that will *get her off your back*," she said.

I waited all night to get in trouble, but trouble didn't come. This was obviously a **new TORTURE** invented by my parents, **making me wait for my punishment.**

While I was on a truth **ROLL**, I called **Smashing Smorgan** and told him that Dad didn't own a luxury boat. Dad didn't even own a rowboat. Smorgan was pretty nice about it. Luckily, something had come up and he was going to be out of the country for the next couple of weeks anyway. **He thanked me for telling him the truth** and said we could still get together soon. I have to admit it felt good to tell the truth, but it was **the only truth all day that didn't get me into trouble.**

After my call, the phone rang again. Mom answered it and yelled for Zoe. It was a pretty short call. When Zoe hung up she *was shaking her head.*

"What's wrong?" I asked.

"Your girlfriend's strange," said Zoe, disappearing into her room.

"**I don't have a girlfriend,**" I shouted as she locked her door and turned up her music. "Zoe?"

I had a **bad feeling** about that phone call.

CHAPTER 10

BLACKMAIL

Thursday, August 6

The next morning I meant to ask Zoe about the phone call, but she'd already left for school.

At recess, we used our **spy skills and followed Rose**. It was the most **boring** spying I'd ever done. Apart from the **GG's** giggling, all we heard was Rose talking about her latest **shopping trip or her skinny dog**, Tiffany, or the newest star her mother was working with. At one point, Rose passed around a *small photo album*. The **GG's looked impressed.**

"**Publicity photos**," Joe whispered to me.

"Ooooh," someone said. "Does your mom know Tim Crude?"

Rose nodded and looked BORED.

"Wow," said another. "Jenny Harggar? This is Jenny Harggars! From the Hard Harggars."

Rose **NODDED** again.

"Have you met all these people?" another girl asked.

"*Sure*," said Rose. "Mother said I should choose someone from this book *to invite to my party*. I haven't decided yet."

"Is it possible **to die** of boredom?" asked Joe. "I'd rather be facing the **unknown terrors** of space **than have to listen to Rose Thornton**."

"Maybe Rose Thornton and Mr. McCafferty aren't plotting against you," said Bec. "Maybe Rose just happened to be walking down your street and just stopped to say hello to him, or something."

"**Maybe**," I said. But I didn't mean it. "I want to know what she's up to."

At lunchtime we found out.

Bec, Joe, and I were sitting under the oak tree. Rose walked up to us with the **school bully**, **Victor Sneddon**.

"Larry, *do you know* my cousin Victor?" she asked.

I nodded. Victor and I had already met. In fact, once he'd eaten dinner at my house.

"Hey, his name isn't Larry," said Victor. "**How's your sister, David?**"

Victor thought my sister was COOL. Zoe thought Victor was **weird**.

Rose crossed her arms. "I'm going to ask some questions and you're going to answer them honestly. The truth. The whole truth."

I thought about Rose's recent visit to Mr. McCafferty. Mom had told Mr. McCafferty about our Boris deal and Mr. McCafferty **must have told Rose**.

"David, I would like you to *tell Victor what you think of him.*"

"What?" I asked.

"Hurry up. I don't have all day," said Victor.

"The truth," warned Rose.

I looked at Victor and TRIED to think of something nice to say.

"I think Victor is very tall," I said. It was true. Victor Sneddon could have been in the world record books for being the tallest kid on the planet.

Rose smirked and Victor frowned.

"What else?" asked Rose.

I looked Victor up and down.

"I think he has very clean shoes," I said. That was also true. I wondered if Victor cleaned his school shoes before coming to school each day. More likely, he had a victim clean them every day.

"What else?" said Rose.

I knew what she wanted me to say, but I wasn't going to. "Rose, are we almost done here?" said Victor.

"What about his hair?" asked Rose.

This was getting **very tricky**. Victor's hair is kind of weird. Like he went for a haircut one day then left in hurry and only got one side cut. Or maybe his mom had attacked it with the CLIPPERS when he was asleep, but only got the side that wasn't on the pillow.

Victor Sneddon had the worst haircut I had ever seen. The trick was not to say that.

"I think Victor's hair is **very shiny**," I said.

"**Very shiny**," Joe agreed.

"Stay out of this, Joe," snapped Rose. "So what about your sister, Larry? What does she think of Victor?"

Victor LOOKED at me. I thought about the short phone call that Zoe had the night before. Suddenly, I realized that the caller had been Rose. I wondered what Zoe and Rose had talked about. **I had a bad feeling about this.**

"This is ridiculous," said Bec with a snort.

The bell rang. I got up, but Victor stopped me. "I'm waiting to hear the answer," he said.

"I'm going to get a teacher," said Bec. Victor grabbed her arm.

"Zoe thinks you're WEIRD," I said.

Victor **dropped** Bec's arm. He looked hurt.

"**Run**!" said Joe.

"Hey, liar!" shouted Victor as Joe, Bec, and I disappeared into the school building. "I know where you live!"

So now I had the **school bully** after me. The truth wasn't all it was cracked up to be.

* * *

After lunch we had some project research time in the library. Rose passed me a note as she walked past on her way to the back shelves.

"I can make Victor stay away, but you'll owe me. Say hi to your dog from me," it read.

I wondered whether it was worse to be in trouble with Victor Sneddon, or to owe Rose Thornton a favor.

Bec, Joe, and I pretended to look for books, but we were **really discussing** what Rose Thornton might do next.

"We need to tell Ms. Stacey," said Bec.

"Tell her what?" I asked. "Tell her that Rose is making me tell the truth?"

"I know that sounds stupid."

"**Shh**," said Joe, finger to his lips.

We stopped talking. On the other side of the bookshelf we **could hear Rose Thornton talking to one of her friends**. Using our best **spy skills**, we walked closer.

"Of course we have a boat, Stephanie. Daddy bought it when I was born. It's called Princess. Anyway, I'm having a *birthday party* there this Saturday. I'm inviting **Smashing Smorgan**. Of course, my mother met him way before **David Baxter** knew him. She gets to meet a whole lot of TV stars through her work. *She's a very good friend.*"

We **CREPT** away and sat down at a computer far away from Rose and her friend.

"Since when has Rose's mom been a very good friend of **Smashing Smorgan**?" asked Bec.

"Since Rose Thornton decided to get back at me," I answered. I didn't believe any of the Thorntons knew **Smashing Smorgan**.

I had figured out Rose's plan. She would call off Victor Sneddon if I got Smashing Smorgan to go to her dumb birthday party. The problem was, Smorgan wasn't even going to be in the country next Saturday. **He definitely wouldn't be at Rose's party.**

I **HOPED** I was wrong about Rose's plans.

CHAPTER 11

THE INVITATION

Thursday, August 6 — Friday, August 7

"Hey, **Dribbles**. Your girlfriend is on the phone," yelled Zoe from the kitchen that night.

This time I knew who she was talking about. I grabbed the phone from Zoe.

"Hello?" I said.

"Hi, Larry." It was Rose. "Did you *read* my note?"

"Yes," I said.

"So, how about it? I call Victor *off and you do me a favor.*" Rose went on about how she could help me if I helped her, and **she wanted Smashing Smorgan at her birthday party** this Saturday.

"Why don't you just invite one of those other famous people that your mom hangs out with?" I asked.

"*I want Smashing Smorgan*. You *owe* me a favor," said Rose.

"Fine," I said finally. "I'll do you one favor."

"*Great*," said Rose.

"But **I can't get Smashing Smorgan** for you this weekend," I said.

It was too late. Rose had already **hung up**.

I had a **BAD feeling**. I was going to have to tell Rose that **Smashing Smorgan** was one favor I couldn't help her out with.

By the time I got to school the next day, it was too late to tell Rose anything. The class was buzzing like a room full of flies. Rose had delivered party invitations to everyone in the class. There was even an invitation on my seat. It had my name on the envelope.

"So **Smorgan's coming to Rose's birthday party**," said Joe. He waved an invitation in the air.

"**No.**"

"What do you mean? The invitation says '**A surprise famous guest**.' I thought it was Smorgan."

"No Smorgan," I said. "I **need to tell Rose right now**. Where is she?"

Joe shrugged. "She rushed in, handed out the invites, and then rushed out again. Said something about **getting ready for the party**."

"But that's a **whole day** away."

Joe shrugged again. "Go figure," he said.

By the end of school that day, everyone was talking about **Rose Thornton's birthday party**. Even Ms. Stacey said she'd come. That wasn't surprising. I just hoped she wouldn't be too **disappointed when Smorgan didn't arrive**.

After school, I called Rose. I had to explain that Smashing Smorgan couldn't come.

"Rose, it's David," I said, when she answered the phone.

"David!" she said, like I was her favorite person. "How *great to hear from you*."

"I need to tell you something," I began.

"How great!" said Rose. "I look forward to seeing you there. I'm looking forward to everyone being there," she said. "Everyone," she whispered angrily before she hung up.

I was in trouble.

CHAPTER 12

TRAPPED

Saturday, August 8

That's how I ended up **locked in the cabin of a luxury boat.**

Our plan was to get to Rose early and let her know that Smorgan wasn't coming. This would give her time to invite another famous person to her party.

Bec's mom dropped Bec, Joe, and me off early at the marina. It took us forever to find the Thorntons' boat. I was looking for a **huge, fancy** boat. But the only boat named Princess was an *old, small, dirty boat.*

"This must be it," I said. "I expected something—"

"**Newer?**" said Joe.

"Richer?" said Bec.

I nodded.

We went onboard. Rose didn't seem to be around.

"We **need to tell her the truth** as soon as she gets here," I said to Joe.

"At least give **her some time to get someone else**," agreed Joe.

Bec called out, "Hey, look what I found."

She was in the boat's cabin. "**Cool**," said Joe. He followed me in.

The room was cool. It was a little smaller than the study at home. On one side was a couch that looked like it might turn into a bed. On another side was a small kitchen. It even had a **tiny fridge**. The place **was really dusty**. There was hardly enough room for the three of us.

"They must not use this cabin," said Bec.

Then the door slammed shut.

Joe rattled the handle, but it wouldn't turn. "**We're locked in**," he whispered.

"Maybe it's kidnappers?" Bec said.

"**Or pirates**," said Joe. "**Or aliens**," he added.

Bec shook her head. "They would have just sucked up the boat into their spaceship," she said. "Anyway, whoever it was is gone now. I don't hear anything."

Ralph's head popped out of Bec's coat pocket. He sniffed the air. Then he ran onto the couch and looked around the cabin.

"What would a **spy do**?" asked Joe.

We looked around the cabin. The window was too small for us to get out of. There was no phone. We thought about sending **Ralph out** of the cabin window with a note tied to his neck. We couldn't be sure he'd find the right people. Our friends and family would never see us again.

Suddenly we heard **footsteps**. It sounded like an army of people. Did our kidnappers come back? There were a few thumps. Then someone SCREECHED. It was crazy.

"Maybe it is aliens," whispered Bec.

A blast of music exploded into the air.

"Rose's party must have started," I said.

"Where did the **kidnappers go**?" asked Joe.

I banged on the door. "Hey!" I yelled. "**Let us out of here!**"

"Maybe there were no kidnappers," said Bec. "Maybe the wind blew the door shut and it got stuck."

"Come on. Help me," I said. Bec and Joe banged on the door with me. But it was no use. The music was really loud. We gave up.

"Let's just wait **until the music stops**," said Joe.

But the music didn't stop. One song blended into the next. A DJ told everyone to dance. My head was pounding. I watched Ralph run along the kitchen sink looking for food. Then I had an idea.

"**Super Spy Ralph to the rescue**," I said loudly.

"What?" said Bec.

"MSV!" I shouted, pointing to Ralph. "If we can get Ralph onto the deck, **someone might see him and realize we're here.**"

"Maybe," said Bec.

There was a GAP under the door. It was big enough for Ralph to squeeze through.

Bec picked up Ralph and looked him in the eye. "Okay, **Ralph**. This is your mission. You need to go under the door and onto the deck. Run around until someone notices you. Do you think you can do that?"

Ralph wasn't paying attention. Bec placed him on the cabin floor and pointed him at the door. "Go, Ralph," she said.

Ralph sat, cleaning his whiskers. Bec pushed him gently toward the gap.

Ralph turned around and ran to the kitchen.

"This is **not going to work**," said Joe. He was chewing on a granola bar.

"Where did you get that?" demanded Bec.

"It was in my pocket," said Joe. "**Hey!**"

I grabbed the granola bar and **broke off a small bite for Ralph.**

"Come on, **Ralph**," I said, holding out the crumb.

Ralph's nose wiggled. I bent down and pushed the crumb under the door.

"Go and get it, **Ralph**," I said.

Ralph wiggled under the door. Then he was gone.

For a while, all we could hear was the **music and loud laughter.**

"Maybe this isn't going to work," said Bec.

Then we heard it. A loud, **high SCREAM**.

"Agent Ralph **has just achieved MSV**," said Joe.

Then there were **more screams and the thud of stamping feet.**

"I don't think **they realized it's Ralph**," said Joe.

Then the cabin door flew open. It was Mrs. Thornton.

"What are you children doing in here? *I told you this was off limits*. I'm looking for a broom," she explained.

"We were **stuck in—**" began Joe, but Bec nudged him.

"Sorry, Mrs. Thornton," said Bec. "We were looking for the bathroom."

We rushed out of the cabin to find Ralph. Half the guests were running around the deck screaming. The other half were laughing. The next thing I knew, Rose Thornton grabbed me by the shoulder.

"Where have you been?" she yelled. "I should have known it was *Bec's stupid rat*. Are you all here?"

I nodded. Then I realized she was talking about **Smashing Smorgan**.

Before I could say a word, Rose made her way to the DJ's microphone and asked everybody to be quiet.

"Turn that music off," she told the DJ.

The girls had stopped running around. Everyone gathered around the DJ platform.

Rose said, "As you all know, I have a special party guest today. He's just a little bit late, but better late than never. *Put your hands together for Smashing Smorgan!"*

People clapped and cheered. The DJ played the theme from "Wicked Wrestling Mania." Then he played it again. People started looking around. Rose had a fake smile on her face.

"David?" she said into the microphone.

The truth was that **Smashing Smorgan** was never coming to Rose Thornton's party. I knew that. And I knew what I had to do.

The truth. The whole truth. And nothing but.

CHAPTER 13

THE LIE

I walked to the microphone.

It was my chance for revenge. To let everyone know about Rose's blackmailing ways. Rose had really gone too far this time. She deserved everything she got.

As I got closer to Rose, I noticed her smile was shaking at the edges. Her hands were SHAKING, too, as she passed me the microphone.

It was her own fault. Rose had plenty of **stars** to choose from. But she wanted Smorgan.

"**Smorgan, Smorgan, Smorgan,**" chanted the crowd.

I looked out and saw Joe and Bec. Bec was holding Ralph and looking worried. Mrs. Thornton was standing near the cabin. She was holding a cell phone to her ear. She didn't seem too interested in being at the party.

"*He's not coming, is he?* You said he would. You *liar!*" whispered Rose. She sounded like she was going to cry.

"**Takes one to know one,**" I said. I looked over at Mrs. Thornton.

Then I thought about the **photos** Rose showed off at school.

Rose Thornton was a liar.

There was no way Rose had her choice of stars for her party. She'd made it up. **That's why she blackmailed me into getting Smorgan to come to her party**. But Smorgan couldn't make it. Now I had to tell the truth. If I didn't tell the truth, I would lose Boris. **I really had no choice.**

"**Smorgan, Smorgan, Smorgan**," chanted the crowd.

"*He's not here, is he,*" whispered Rose. Tears filled her eyes. I thought I would be happy to see Rose sad. Rose was crying on her birthday. Mrs. Thornton was still talking on the phone. She wasn't going to rescue Rose. I looked into Rose's eyes. **She was a liar, just like me.**

"Thanks everyone. Thank you," I shouted into the microphone.

The crowd HUSHED.

"I'm afraid I have some bad news," I began.

I found a sheet of paper in my pocket and **waved** it in the air. "I have a message here. It was delivered by Smorgan's driver this morning. I'll read it for you. '**To my good friend Rose Thornton**. I'm very sorry that I cannot make it to your birthday party this afternoon. I have to leave the country. Suddenly. I would much rather be at your party than earning lots of money, but my manager won't let me. Anyway, have a great birthday. I'll see you when I get back. **Smorgan**.'"

The crowd started **booing**.

"Hang on, I'm not done. 'Please say hello to all your friends from me and tell them that they're invited to the Wrestling Mania's end of season party.'"

The crowd **erupted into cheers**.

I continued, "But to make up for no Smorgan, Mrs. Thornton has organized a treasure hunt. It starts now. I think you'll really like the prize. Happy hunting!"

Mrs. Thornton, who was finally off the phone, looked bewildered.

"We haven't organized a treasure hunt," said Rose. She frowned. "And where's Smorgan?"

"Smorgan couldn't make it. I tried to tell you. I'd get your mom to find a prize pretty quickly," I said back.

"Did Smorgan really send that note?" she asked.

I shook my head.

"So you just lied," confirmed Rose. "*You could have told the truth but you lied. And when your parents find out . . . your dog, David!*"

I **SHRUGGED**.

"I'm calling *off Victor,*" said Rose. "Even though you didn't deliver Smorgan."

"**Don't do me any favors, Rose,**" I said.

I wished I was at **home**, spending my last day with Boris.

CHAPTER 14

WHISKERS

Bec won the treasure hunt. Mrs. Thornton found a prize in her car's trunk. There was a Hard Harggers gift pack, including a T-shirt, a drink bottle, some posters, and lip gloss. There were also a couple of CDs and DVDs. Bec wasn't happy, though. Neither were Joe or I. All we could think about was **Boris leaving**.

"Just **don't tell them**," said Joe. "How are your parents going to find out?"

"My mom is **friends with Mrs. Thornton. She'll find out**," I said.

Bec's mom dropped me off at home. **I tried to sneak inside.**

"Gran's here," called out Mom as the door clicked quietly shut.

Great. Gran must be staying for dinner. The thing that would really make my day would be Mom's **vegetarian loaf**. If we had to eat that, I would have to tell her the truth.

The **truth** was that I really, really, really don't like it.

I walked into the dining room to find Mom and Gran looking at some paper spread out over the dining table. Gran had her genealogy charts out again. Genealogy is one of **Gran's hobbies**. It's finding out who your grandparents were, and their grandparents.

But Gran can't remember our names. She'll recite her whole family tree before she gets our names right.

"Daniel!" said Gran.

"It's **David**," I heard Mom whisper.

"*David*," repeated Gran, pointing her finger onto the page in front of her. "*David Mortimore Baxter.* That name was *good enough* for your grandfather."

This was one of Gran's favorite speeches. It could go on and on and on. The trick was to look a little interested **but not too interested**. I usually just stared at the whiskers on Gran's chin.

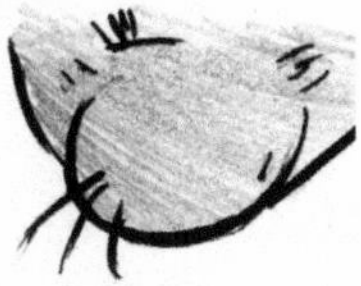

I heard Boris scratching at the back door to get inside. He must have heard my voice.

I just wanted one more afternoon with **Boris** before **I had to give him up.**

"What are you *staring at, boy?*" Gran asked suddenly. I stopped thinking about Boris.

"**Well?**" asked Gran. Her white whiskers were shining in the sunlight. I couldn't help staring. They hung down below her chin **like a goat's beard.** Make that a granny goat.

"**Not by the hair on my chinny chin chin,**" I whispered.

Mom **grabbed the dining table** like she needed help standing up.

"*What?* Louder. Speak clearly," said Gran. "Your grandfather had that habit. He was always talking into his beard."

Mom shook her head slowly. I knew what she wanted. I should tell the truth. I should let her know how hard it had been for me over the last week.

Gran **poked me in the ribs**. She had really strong fingers.

"I said sisters. I was wondering if you looked like your sisters," I said.

Mom sat down with a **jolt**.

"Well, of course I do!" cried Gran. "Now look here."

Mom interrupted Gran with an excuse about getting dinner ready and then made a big show about getting me to help her.

In the hallway Mom turned to me. She laid a hand on my shoulder.

"**David, we need to talk. Now!**" she said.

Mom marched me into the study, where Dad was playing a game of Solitaire on the computer.

"Sit down, Davey," said Mom. "Rose Thornton called just before you came home."

You had to hand it to Rose. **She was always first with the news.**

"She told me what you did today."

"She did?"

"She told me everything. It was very brave of her to make that call."

"I lied."

"She said you were very kind," said Mom. "I think you were, too."

What?

"And your father and I have an apology to make."

"We do?" asked Dad.

"You do?" I asked. Dad and I looked at each other.

"David, the other night I was very angry when you pretended to be sick. You lied about being sick and we found out. It was only fair that you should be punished for lying. Don't you agree?" Mom asked.

I nodded.

"However, my punishment was . . ."

"Unfair?" suggested Dad.

"Too HARSH," continued Mom. "**Boris is part of this family**. Of course I would NEVER send him away."

"You wouldn't?" I looked up at my parents.

"Who else would want that stupid dog?" said Dad gruffly.

"Is this because of Gran's whiskers?" I asked.

Mom ignored my question. "I think our punishment wasn't realistic," she said. "I've noticed that you've kept your part of our bargain this week. You've been telling the whole truth. I think it's been getting you into trouble."

"You're not wrong," I said.

"I think we've both realized this week that sometimes we need to bend the truth. We all do it. Even if it's pretending Rose Thornton is good friends with Smashing Smorgan. Even if it's just pretending that we're not staring at Grandma Baxter's chin hair."

"So I can't tell Gran that I was staring at her whiskers?" I asked.

"NO, David," said Mom.

"So Boris is staying?" I asked.

"YES, David," said Dad.

"Do I still have to eat that new cereal, Mom?" I asked.

"Yes, David," said Mom.

"Can I go tell Boris that he's staying?"

"Yes, David. Then wash up. It's almost dinner time," said Mom.

Before I rushed out the door, I asked, "What's for dinner?"

"**Vegetarian loaf,**" said Mom.

I looked at Dad. He didn't like veggie loaf almost as much as I didn't. He raised his eyebrows at me.

I looked Mom straight in the eye.

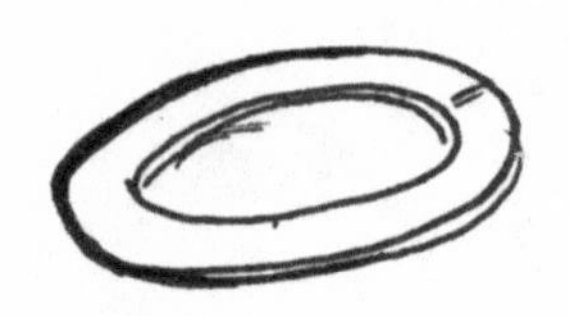

"**Great!**" I said. "I can't wait!"

So here's the thing. **Knowing when to tell and when not to tell lies is very tricky.**

And that's the **HONEST truth**.

The End

When Karen Tayleur was growing up, her father told her many stories about his own childhood. These stories continued to grow. She says, "I always enjoyed the retelling, and wanted to create a character who had the same abilities with 'bending the truth.'" And David Mortimore Baxter was born! Karen lives in Australia with her husband, two children, two cats, and one dog.

Brann Garvey grew up in the great state of Iowa, where he studied art and visual communications. He graduated from the Minneapolis College of Art & Design with a degree in illustration. Brann is usually found with one or more of the following: a pencil in his hand, a comic book, a remote for watching DVDs, or his pet kitty, Iggy. When the weather is nice, Brann likes to play disc golf, and he proudly points out that Iowa is one of the world's centers for the sport. Iggy does not play.

blackmail (BLAK-mayl)—to try to force a person to pay or do something by threatening to tell a secret

coincidence (koh-IN-si-duhnss)—the unplanned happening of two events at the same time

defenseless (di-FENSS-lehss)—unable to protect

demolish (di-MOL-ish)—to tear down completely; wreck

harsh (HARSH)—cruel; severe

investigate (in-VESS-tuh-gate)—to examine carefully in a search for information

maximum (MAK-suh-mum)—highest or greatest possible

pant (PANT)—to breathe in short, quick gasps

pound (POUND)—a place for keeping lost animals

rations (RASH-unz)—small portions of food for special times, such as camping or military work

revenge (ri-VENJ)—to do injury or harm in return for injury or harm done to one

strategy (STRAT-uh-jee)—a clever plan of action

vital (VYE-tuhl)—important

1. What is the point that this author makes about telling the truth? Do you agree or disagree? Explain your thinking.

2. On page 82, what do you think of Mom's explanation about telling the truth versus bending the truth? How do YOU decide when to tell the truth and when to bend the truth?

3. How did you feel when David gets in trouble for telling the truth? Explain.

4. How does Rose and David's relationship change throughout the book? Give examples. How do they feel about each other at the end of the book?

1. Do you believe in telling the truth, the whole truth, and nothing but the truth? Explain why or why not.

2. When is a lie a lie? Are there different kinds of lies? Write a list of all the different kinds of lies (small ones, big ones, strange ones, silly ones) that you can think of.

3. Explain, in writing, what it means to blackmail someone. Make up your own examples or use those from the book.

More fun

David Mortimore Baxter

David is a great kid, but he has one big problem — he can't stop talking. These wildly humorous stories, told by David himself, will show readers just how much trouble a boy and his mouth can get into, whether he's making promises to become class president or bragging that he's best friends with the world's most famous wrestler. David is amiable, engaging, cool, and smart enough to realize that growing up is the biggest adventure of all.

with David!
ADMIT ONE
ADMIT ONE
Promises!
MORTIMORE
THE SECRET LIFE OF DAVID MORTIMORE BAXTER
Secrets!
DAVID MORTIMORE BAXTER
BY KAREN TAYLEUR
DIARY

WAIT!
DON'T close the book!
There's MORE!
FIND MORE:
Games
Puzzles
Heroes
Villains
Authors
Illustrators at...
www.capstonekids.com
Still want MORE?
Find cool websites and more books like this one at www.Facthound.com.
Just type in the Book ID: 1598890786
and you're ready to go!

EXIT
KEEP OUT
THE BOOK OF SECRET NOTES
FOR SALE
S
ORANGE JUICE
P
GRAPE
ADMIT ONE
EXIT
MEOW MEIN

SLOW
SCHOOL
EXIT
REPORT CARD
ADMIT ONE
ORANGE JUICE
MEOW MEON
GRAPE
P
POLICE
SMASHING
THE BOOK OF SECRET NOTES
Property of KITSCH ELEMENTARY